MAX and ANN'S FIELD DAY

In Bloom

By Cecilia Minden

CHAPTER 1

It is Field Day. Ann has a tennis match.

Ann hits the ball up high.

Jen hits it into the net.

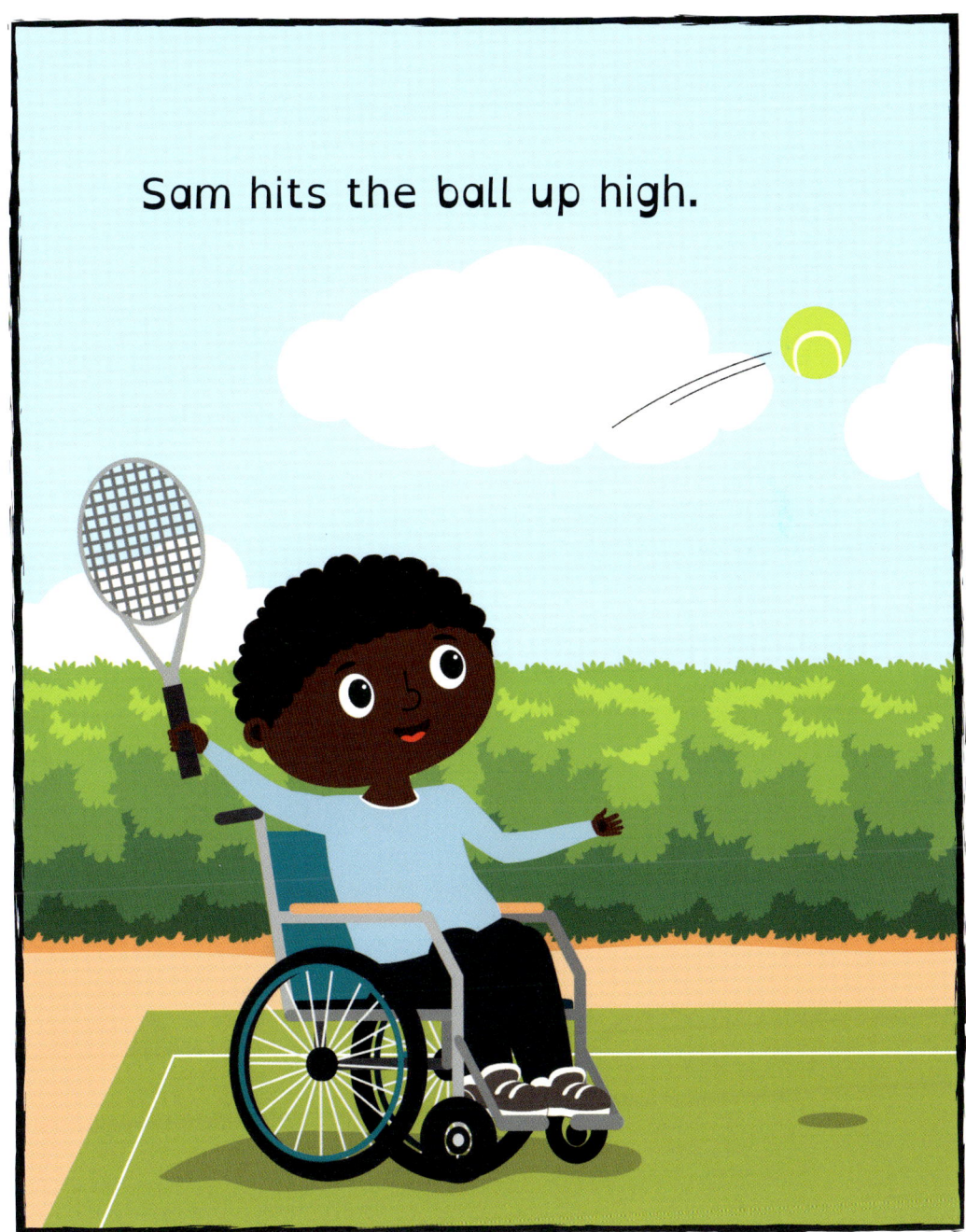

Ted hits it into the net.

Ann and Sam win!

CHAPTER 2

The big class race is next. Ann and Jen clap hands. Kids stretch. Max and Sam grin.

Ann can run fast.

The race is on!

Can Max catch up?

Kids rush up the path.

WORD LIST

sight words

a	high	tennis	they
Day	into	the	Who
Field	race	The	

consonant digraphs

/th/
path

/l/ ll
ball
will

/s/ ss
class

/ch/ tch
catch
match
stretch

/n/ nn
Ann

/sh/ sh
rush

112 WORDS

It is Field Day. Ann has a tennis match.
Ann hits the ball up high.
Ann hits it in.
Jen hits the ball.
Jen hits it into the net.
Sam hits the ball up high.
Sam hits it in.
Ted hits the ball.
Ted hits it into the net.
Ann and Sam win!

The big class race is next. Ann and Jen clap hands.
Kids stretch. Max and Sam grin.
Who will win? Kids must run fast.
Max can run fast.
Ann can run fast.
The race is on!
Kids run as fast as they can.
Ann sprints fast!
Can Max catch up?
Kids rush up the path.
Field Day is fun!

Published in the United States of America by Cherry Lake Publishing Group
Ann Arbor, Michigan
www.cherrylakepublishing.com

Illustrated by Rachael McLean
Book Designer: Melinda Millward

Graphic Element Credits: Cover, multiple interior pages: © memej/Shutterstock, © Eka Panova/Shutterstock, © Pand P Studio/Shutterstock, © PRebellion Works/Shutterstock

Copyright © 2025 by Cherry Lake Publishing Group
All rights reserved. No part of this book may be reproduced or utilized in
any form or by any means without written permission from the publisher.

Cherry Blossom Press is an imprint of Cherry Lake Publishing Group.

Library of Congress Cataloging-in-Publication Data

Names: Minden, Cecilia, author. | McLean, Rachael, illustrator.
Title: Max and Ann's field day / written by Cecilia Minden ; illustrated by Rachael McLean.
Description: Ann Arbor, MI : Cherry Blossom Press, 2024. | Series: In bloom | This book focuses on consonant digraphs. | Audience: Grades 2-3 | Summary: "What games will Max and Ann play during Field Day? Find out in this decodable chapter book. This book uses sequenced phonics skills and sight words to help developing readers. Original illustrations guide readers through the story. Author Cecilia Minden, PhD, a literacy consultant and former director of the Language and Literacy program at Harvard Graduate School of Education developed the specific format for this series"-- Provided by publisher.
Identifiers: LCCN 2024009609 | ISBN 9781668947791 (hardcover) | ISBN 9781668946404 (paperback) | ISBN 9781668949313 (ebook) | ISBN 9781668953877 (pdf)
Subjects: LCSH: Readers (Primary) | English language--Consonants--Juvenile literature. | Outdoor games--Juvenile literature. | Reading--Phonetic method--Juvenile literature. | LCGFT: Readers (Publications).
Classification: LCC PE1119.2 .M5658 2024 | DDC 428.6/2--dc23/eng/20240301
LC record available at https://lccn.loc.gov/2024009609

Cherry Lake Publishing Group would like to acknowledge the work of the
Partnership for 21st Century Learning, a Network of Battelle for Kids.
Please visit Battelle for Kids online for more information.

Printed in the United States of America

Cecilia Minden is the former director of the Language and Literacy Program at Harvard Graduate School of Education. She earned her PhD in Reading Education at the University of Virginia. Dr. Minden has written extensively for early readers. She is passionate about matching children to the very book they need to improve their skills and progress to a deeper understanding of all the wonder books can hold.

Note from publisher: Websites change regularly, and their future contents are outside of our control. Supervise children when conducting any recommended online searches for extended learning opportunities.